D0241934

Withdrawn from Stock
Dublin City Public Libraries

THE GRUMPY GUEST

Peter Bently
Duncan Beedie

Hello! This is a story about four friendly monsters who live on Planet Pok.

This is **Nid**.

This is **Gop**.

This is **San**.

This is **Pem Pem**.

They have a funny way of talking. It's called **Monsters' Nonsense**.

See if you can read what they are saying. Ready?

Leabharlanna Poibli Chathair Bhaile Átha Cliath

Dublin City Public Libraries

The monsters were playing football together when an expensive new spaceship arrived.

Gulk!

Thregbatt!

It was Huff Huff, Pem Pem's bossy cousin, who lived on Planet Pag.

PEMBROKE BRANCH TEL. 6689575

Huff Huff had decided to visit Pem Pem for a week. He ordered Pem Pem to make him some lunch at once.

Crink lubwiff quee!

Pem Pem baked a tasty blue broccoli pie. But Huff Huff demanded speckled sprouts instead.

Pem Pem had to go all the way to the top of the Speckled Sprout Tree to get them.

Trixerb breft!

Yup grolfer pethramm!

After lunch, Pem Pem and his friends wanted to carry on playing football.

Mandott plut plut zigger!

Sallip murt weng.

Huff Huff didn't like football and wanted to have a spaceship race instead. He made such a fuss that the other monsters gave in.

Huff Huff's new spaceship was much faster than everyone else's, so he won easily.

Lippee hippee!

He didn't stop boasting for the rest of the day.

That night, Huff Huff insisted on sleeping in Pem Pem's bed. Pem Pem had to sleep on the sofa.

Thonk ronk!

Huff Huff snored so loudly that the cave shook and Pem Pem didn't get a wink of sleep.

In the morning, Huff Huff greedily gobbled all of Pem Pem's Cosmic Curly Cornflakes. There was nothing left for poor Pem Pem.

After breakfast, Huff Huff wanted to see something exciting.

Pem Pem and his friends showed him the Emerald Rocks and the Fizzy Fountain. Huff Huff said they were boring.

Fam grench thrisker!

Nid went to find a snack, so the others took Huff Huff to see the Blue Bouncy Boulders.

Grom habluff brundery!

Strench!

Huff Huff yawned and said Planet Pag was more exciting. He really was a VERY rude monster.

Huff Huff spotted a tunnel. It looked much more interesting than the Blue Bouncy Boulders.

Before anyone could stop him, he headed inside.

The tunnel went deeper
and deeper underground.

In the dark, Pem Pem bashed both his heads.

Krogg!

Then Huff Huff spotted something, so
Gop switched on her Flying Flashlight.
A big green rock was blocking the tunnel.

Huff Huff wanted to try to move the rock.
The bossy monster ordered Pem Pem, San
and Gop to push it as hard as they could.

But the rock wouldn't budge. Huff Huff told everyone to move out of the way.

Hurtig scrip tazz botchen!

He took a long run up — and charged towards the rock at full speed.

Just as Huff Huff reached
the green rock, it rolled out
of the way! He was running
too fast to stop.

Nucknuck
droost!

He hurtled past the rock into a
huge cave – and straight into a pool
of sticky, brown gloop. SPLOP!

Huff Huff had fallen into the underground Toffee Lake. He was very cross. Pem Pem and the others tried not to giggle as they pulled him out.

Joppack chonk!

In a dark corner of the cave, the green rock moved again. It let out a grunt.

Eek! Huff Huff yelped in fright. It wasn't a rock. It was a scary underground monster!

Terrified, he ran straight back to his spaceship.

Scraff scraff kulch!

Pem Pem and the others watched as
Huff Huff zoomed back to Planet Pag.

Thrambit
nedding
stroft!

Then they heard something coming
from the tunnel behind them.

It wasn't a scary underground monster at all. It was Nid! He had nipped down to the Toffee Lake for a snack and had fallen asleep in the tunnel.

The monsters all laughed.

Pem Pem laughed most of all. He was glad his bossy, greedy cousin had gone home.

Helving chister quibb!

He invited the monsters back to his cave for a special treat. A blue broccoli and toffee pie!

Reading with your monsters!

Monsters' Nonsense is all about having fun whilst learning the skills of reading. If children have fun reading, they'll want to do it more.

What helps children with their reading?

Phonics: the ability to sound out (decode) words that they don't know.

Reading comprehension: to read for meaning so that they can understand and enjoy the story.

The *Monsters' Nonsense* series is designed to support these skills to help children become successful, happy readers and to encourage a positive, shared reading experience.

The adult reader (or reading mentor) reads the main narrative – supporting reading comprehension and bringing the story alive.

The child reads the Monsters' Nonsense in the speech bubbles. These are 'non-words' to help them practise their decoding skills at a level that is right for them. It's important that your child knows that these 'non-words' are not real words and have no meaning.

More monster fun

Monster Questions Ask your child some questions about the story. For example, where does Huff Huff live? Why didn't Pem Pem sleep very well? Why was Nid in the tunnel? In what way was Huff Huff bossy and rude? Think about the Toffee Lake. Can you describe it using three adjectives?

Adding Adjectives Find adjectives in the text. Make a list of them on some paper or a whiteboard. Then, make up some fun new sentences. Each sentence must contain at least three of the adjectives.

Syllable Detective Ask your child to look through the monster language in the speech bubbles and show you an example of words containing one syllable, two syllables and three syllables. Ask them to clap or stamp the syllables as they say the word. You can repeat this activity using the story text too.

Words within Monster Words Sometimes words can be easier to read and spell if you break them up. Some words have smaller words inside. Go through the monsters' nonsense words with your child and see if you can see one (or more!) real words hiding. For example: threg**bat**t, man**dot**t, br**under**y.

Phonics glossary

blend to blend individual sounds together to pronounce a word, e.g. s-n-a-p blended together reads snap.

digraph two letters representing one sound, e.g. sh, ch, th, ph.

grapheme a letter or a group of letters representing one sound, e.g. t, b, sh, ch, igh, ough (as in 'though').

High Frequency Words (HFW) are words that appear most often in printed materials. They may not be decodable using phonics (or too advanced) but they are useful to learn separately by sight to develop fluency in reading.

phoneme a single identifiable sound, e.g. the letter 't' represents just one sound and the letters 'sh' represent just one sound.

segment to split up a word into its individual phonemes in order to spell it, e.g. the word 'cat' has three phonemes: /c/, /a/, /t/.

vowel digraph two vowels which together make one sound, e.g. ai, oo, ow.

Remember to praise your child and enjoy the shared reading experience.

Quarto is the authority on a wide range of topics.

Quarto educates, entertains and enriches the lives of our readers—enthusiasts and lovers of hands-on living.

www.quartoknows.com

Editor: Emily Pither
Designer: Verity Clark
Consultant: Carolyn Clarke

© 2018 Quarto Publishing plc

First published in 2018 by QED Publishing, an imprint of The Quarto Group. The Old Brewery, 6 Blundell Street, London N7 9BH, United Kingdom. T (0)20 7700 6700 F (0)20 7700 8066 www.QuartoKnows.com

All rights reserved. No part of this publication may be reproduced, stored in a retrieval system, or transmitted in any form or by any means, electronic, mechanical, photocopying, recording, or otherwise, without the prior permission of the publisher, nor be otherwise circulated in any form of binding or cover other than that in which it is published and without a similar condition being imposed on the subsequent purchaser.

A catalogue record for this book is available from the British Library.

ISBN 978 1 78493 974 8

Manufactured in Dongguan, China TL 012018

9 8 7 6 5 4 3 2 1

FSC
www.fsc.org

MIX
Paper from responsible sources
FSC® C104723